Tee hee!

Squash the Spider!

For Chris, Ian, Mark,
Richard and Roger.
Great with computers,
useless with spiders!

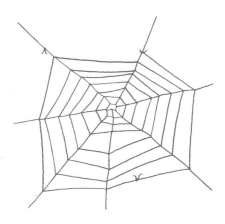

A DAVID FICKLING BOOK

Published by David Fickling Books
an imprint of Random House Children's Books
a division of Random House, Inc.
New York
Copyright © 2003 by Nick Ward

Published simultaneously in Canada by Random House of Canada Limited, Toronto, and in
Great Britain by David Fickling Books, an imprint of Random House Children's Books

www.randomhouse.com/kids

Library of Congress Cataloging-in-Publication Data is available upon request.

ISBN 0-385-75017-X

MANUFACTURED IN CHINA
June 2004

10 9 8 7 6 5 4 3 2 1

First American Edition

Squash the Spider!

Nick Ward

David Fickling Books

OXFORD · NEW YORK

High up on the ceiling Squash
the Spider was waiting to pounce!
Billy came in to watch T.V. and
eat his supper.

He settled in front of the telly.

Billy was just about to
take a great big bite out of
his sandwich when . . .

"Yuck!" screamed Billy.
"Mum, **SQUASH the SPIDER!**"

But when Billy's mum rushed in, the spider was gone.

After supper it was Billy's bedtime. "Goodnight Mum," he called. Billy snuggled under his covers and was soon fast asleep.

In a secret hiding place, Squash was already snoring, dreaming up his next trick.

At school the next day, Billy and his friends sat down on the story mat. "Ssh! Let's start with a nice quiet story," whispered the teacher, opening her book. "All about . . ."

"Eek!" squealed the teacher.
"SQUASH the SPIDER!"

Once upon a time in a land
far far away, lived a
princess. But the
...sad because
...her up
...in a tall...
In a co...
a spider sat sp...

Squash jumped!
"Yuck!" cried the whole class.
"Where's he gone?"
But Squash had completely
disappeared!

At lunchtime, Billy was in the
playground with his friends.
"I'm not really scared of spiders,"
he explained. "I was only pretending."

"Me too," said Jo.
"Who wants a crisp?"
"What flavor?"
asked Billy reaching into the bag.

Spider flavor!

"Yuck!" screamed Billy.
"SQUASH the SPIDER!"

Jo grabbed Squash. "I'm not scared," she said. "Look . . ."
Jo opened her fingers. Squash wriggled his long spidery legs and . . .

Whizz! He shot straight up Jo's sleeve.

Yuck! Get him out!

Pop!

Jo wriggled and squiggled and flapped . . .

. . . And Squash flew out of Jo's other sleeve and tumbled to the ground.

Tee hee!

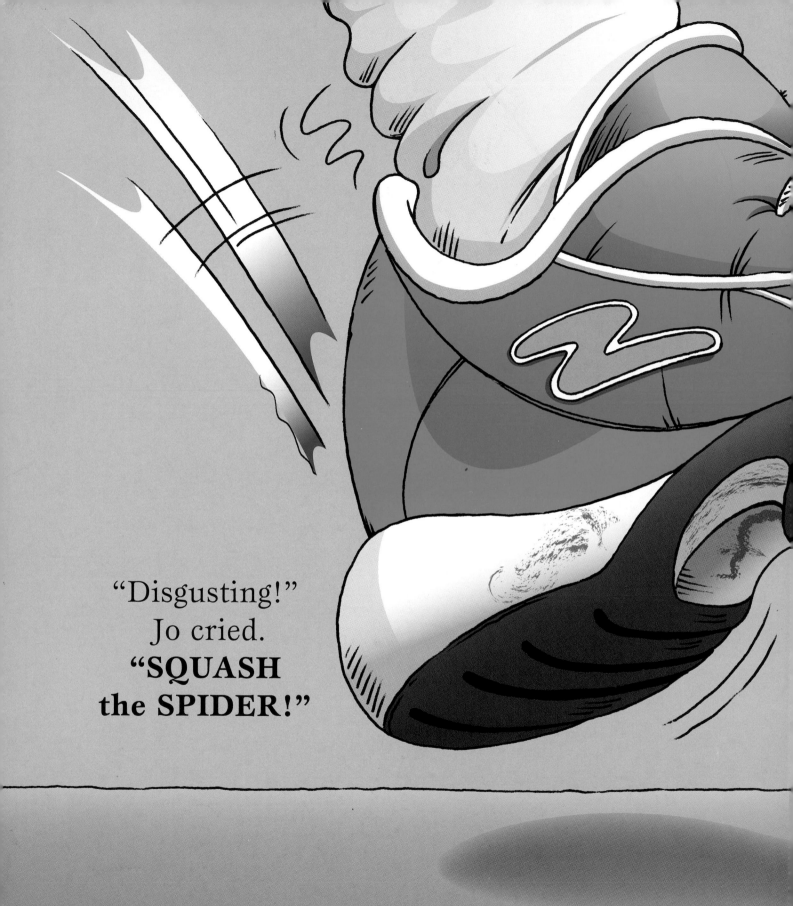

"Disgusting!"
Jo cried.
**"SQUASH
the SPIDER!"**

STO

"Phew! That was close!" gasped Squash on the way home. "But I've learned my lesson. I will never ever ever scare anyone again!"
"Promise?" asked Billy.
"Promise!" said Squash.

And from that day on, Squash the spider never shouted "Boo!" and never ever scared anyone again.

12

SPIDER LANE

Well, almost never.